This Walker book belongs to:

_____

_____

_____

To my sister, Anna

First published 2002 by Walker Books Ltd
87 Vauxhall Walk, London SE11 5HJ

This edition published 2004

2 4 6 8 10 9 7 5 3

Printed in China

British Library Cataloguing in Publication Data:
a catalogue record for this book is available
from the British Library

ISBN 978-1-8442-8466-5

www.walker.co.uk

How Kind!

Mary Murphy

WALKER BOOKS
AND SUBSIDIARIES
LONDON · BOSTON · SYDNEY

Hen gave Pig an egg.

"How kind!" said Pig.

Pig kept the egg safe and warm. "Hen is so kind," he thought. "I would like to do something kind too."

Pig gave Rabbit a carrot.
"This is for you," said Pig.

"How kind!" said Rabbit.

"Pig is so kind," thought Rabbit. "I will do something kind too." He picked some flowers.

How kind!" said Cow

"Rabbit is very kind," thought Cow. "How can I be kind too?"

She gave Cat some milk.

"HOW kind!" said Cat.

Cow is so kind, thought Cat. "I want to be kind too." She looked for Puppy. "Let's play your favourite game, Puppy," said Cat.

"How kind!" said Puppy.

They chased round

and round.

"Cat is so kind," thought Puppy. "I want to be kind too."

Puppy fetched a stick. He scratched Pig's back. "How kind!" said Pig.

"Would you like to see my egg, Puppy?

Puppy looked
at the egg.
"It's nice," he said.
"What is it for?"

They brought the chick
back to Hen, and
Hen said,
"How kind!"

Other books by Mary Murphy

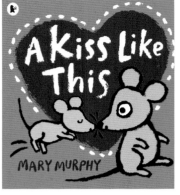

ISBN 978-1-4063-4538-4

ISBN 978-1-4063-5994-7

ISBN 978-1-4063-6588-7

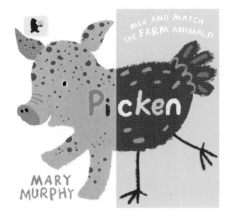

ISBN 978-1-4063-7137-6

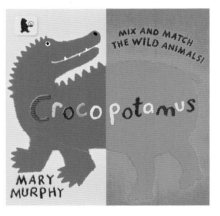

ISBN 978-1-4063-5789-9

ISBN 978-1-4063-5378-5

ISBN 978-1-4063-4828-6

Available from all good booksellers

www.walker.co.uk